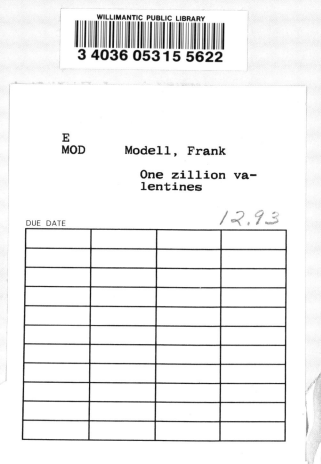

FRANK MODELL

One Zillion Valentines

GREENWILLOW BOOKS ❤ New York

Library of Congress Cataloging in Publication Data
Modell, Frank.   One zillion valentines.
Summary: When Marvin shows Milton how to make valentines,
they decide to make one for each person in their neighborhood.
[1. Valentines—Fiction. 2. St. Valentine's
Day—Fiction] I. Title.
PZ7.M7140n   [E]   81-2215
ISBN 0-688-00565-9   AACR2
ISBN 0-688-00569-1 (lib. bdg.)

One of Marvin's favorite
days was Valentine's Day.

"If I had a lot of money, I'd buy all those valentines," said Marvin.
"That's silly," said Milton.
"You don't even have a girl."

"Valentines aren't just for girls.
Valentines are for everybody,"
said Marvin. "If I were a pilot,
I'd draw a great big one in the sky."

"No one ever sent *me* a valentine,"
said Milton.

"That's because you never send any,"
said Marvin. "If you don't send any,
you don't get any."
"I never have any money," said Milton.
"Valentines cost money."

"You don't have to buy valentines,
you can make them. All you do
is get a lot of paper and draw
a big heart like this," said Marvin.
"I can do that," said Milton.

"Anyone can do it," said Marvin. "I bet
we could make a zillion valentines.
One for everybody in the neighborhood."
"A zillion is a lot of valentines," said
Milton. "We better start right away."

Milton went to his house and got out his
paint set, his scissors, and colored paper.

Marvin went to his house and got out his
crayons, colored pencils, and a lot of paper.

They made valentines with big hearts, little hearts,
skinny hearts, fat hearts, polka dot hearts,

striped hearts, red hearts on white paper,
and white hearts on red paper.

"Now what do we do?" said Milton.
"We send them to everybody," said Marvin.
"That's silly," said Milton.
"We'll need a zillion stamps."

"No we won't," said Marvin. "We'll put them under people's doors. I'll take this side of the street and you take the other."

The next morning everybody in the neighborhood

was surprised to find a valentine under the door.

"We have lots left over," said Milton.
"I guess we made too many."

"No we didn't," said Marvin.
"People like to send valentines too.
They don't just like to get them."

"They are all gone," said Milton.
"Great," said Marvin.

"Maybe," said Milton. "But I bet
we don't get a valentine from anyone."
"Sure we do," said Marvin.
"Follow me."

"A happy Valentine's Day to you, Milton."

"A happy Valentine's Day to you, Marvin."

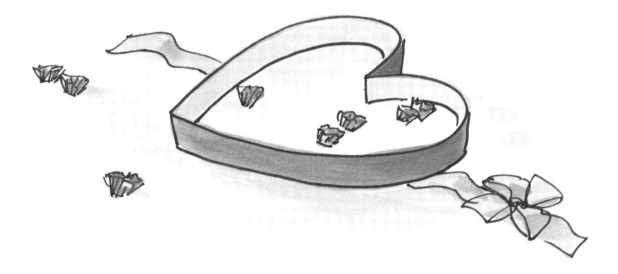